TERRELL PINA

Inheritance Protocol

"Unlock the cube. Unleash the truth."

Contents

Prologue 1

1 Ashes and Acid Rain 3

2 Executor 6

3 The Voice in the Cube 10

4 Coordinates 13

5 Watched 17

6 Exit Node 21

7 The Pinefield Perimeter 25

8 Threshold Test 28

9 Breach Window Begins 32

10 The First Door 36

11 Substructure 39

12 Memory Seed 42

13 The Voice That Remains 46

14 The Failed Door 50

15 Ghost Loop 54

16 Echo of the Architect 57

17 Burial Coordinates 60

18 Error: External Alignment 63

19 Surface Override 66

20 Pulse Event 69

21 The Divergence Pattern 72

22 Inheritance Conflict 75

23 Null Sequence Recognition 78

24 Control Core: Locked 81

25 Signal Bloom 84

26 False Containment   87
27 Echo Threshold   90
28 Overflow Directive   93
29 The Breach Wasn't Physical   97
30 The Lock Reversed   100
31 The Body Wasn't the Goal   103
32 Marcus Lied About Containment   106
33 The Contact Field   110
34 He Was the Broadcast   114
35 Something Answers   118
36 Site-12 Is No Longer Listening   122
37 Marcus's Silence   125
38 The Failed Body   128
39 Echo Reboots   132
40 You Were the Replacement   136
41 Static Awakening   139
42 Marcus's Final Layer   142
43 The Loop Can't Hold Both   145
44 He Reached Back First   148
45 Restart Condition   151

Prologue

**Marcus Cross – Undated Recording
 [Site-09 – Sub level 5, Memory Vault]**

Begin log.

They'll say I died quietly. In my sleep. Peacefully.

I didn't.

This message isn't for the government. It isn't for my daughter. It's not even for the men watching me from across the street right now.

It's for the next one.

The cube found you. That means the protocol has started again—whether I wanted it to or not.

I told myself I buried it deep enough. That no one would ever come back. That blood would forget.

But memory doesn't rot like flesh. It waits. It grows down instead of up.

If you're hearing this, you already feel it. That low hum. That pressure in the air before the lights flicker. You think you're being watched?

You're not wrong.

You have three days before the first breach window. That's how long it'll take to open again. After that, I can't protect you. No one can.

I broke the door to keep something *in*.
    You're going to be asked to open it again.

And you will.

Because curiosity is louder than fear.
    And blood always remembers its source.

1

Ashes and Acid Rain

The rain hissed against the funeral home's windows like static—relentless, sharp, industrial. It didn't fall like water; it felt corrosive, like the city had been exhaling poison all day and the sky finally gave up holding it in.

Aiden Cross stepped in late. The door whispered shut behind him. The place smelled like fake roses and varnish. Black suits, black umbrellas, and one framed photograph near the casket—his grandfather staring out of it with the same cold stare Aiden remembered from childhood.

He stood at the back, hood up, sneakers dripping onto the carpet. His hair was still wet from the run over—he hadn't brought an umbrella. Didn't really see the point.

A voice was murmuring up front—someone giving a eulogy, though Aiden wasn't paying attention. Most of the chairs were full, which was weird. His grandfather had been reclusive, borderline mythological. Aiden barely remembered him as anything more than a sharp face and a bitter voice in a Christmas phone call once.

The people here didn't seem like friends. They didn't cry. They didn't smile.

They just… watched. One man in particular—a tall guy with a shaved head and tinted glasses—kept glancing back. Aiden looked away quickly.

He shifted his weight, hands in pockets. His hoodie was soaked through, but he didn't care. He stared at the polished casket up front, trying to feel something. Grief, maybe. Anger. Instead, there was just a dull throb of curiosity and a vague sense of being in the wrong room.

Flash—

A memory. Ten years ago. Sitting in a stiff armchair while a much older man handed him a wooden puzzle box and said, "If you can solve that, you're already smarter than your father."

Aiden had solved it in four minutes. The man hadn't smiled. Just took the box back and muttered, "Try again when it matters."

Back in the room now, someone coughed. A woman in a tight black dress dabbed her eyes but wasn't crying. Not really. Just going through the motions.

Aiden moved toward the side exit quietly, already done with the whole thing. No one stopped him. The second he pushed through the side door, the sound of rain doubled—louder, closer. It was coming down in sheets, stinging his skin. He tugged his hood back up.

Then—

"Aiden." A woman's voice. Flat. Unfriendly.

He froze halfway down the steps. A woman in a charcoal-gray coat stepped out of the shadows near the corner of the building. Tall, composed, maybe early 40s. Sharp cheekbones. Black gloves.

"I'm Evelyn Cross," she said. "Your aunt."

He blinked. "I don't have an aunt."

"You do now. Or at least, I exist. And I'm the executor of your grandfather's estate." She reached into her coat slowly, like someone trained not to startle others.

Aiden instinctively took a step back.

She held out a black case—sleek, rectangular, metallic. No branding. No latch.

"He left this for you. No one else."
  She pressed it into his hands before he could object.

He looked down at it. The surface was warm. Not like metal. Almost like skin.

"What is it?"

"Open it when you're alone," she said. "Some things should only be seen by blood."

And without another word, Evelyn turned and disappeared around the side of the building.

Aiden stood alone in the rain, the case pulsing slightly in his hands.

2

Executor

The black case was warmer now, like it had a pulse of its own. Aiden didn't move.

Rain beaded down his sleeves and ran into his cuffs as he stared at the spot where Evelyn had vanished. Around the side of the building—gone, like she'd been absorbed by the shadows.

He glanced down at the object in his hands again. No seams. No buttons. Just matte, black surface and a subtle hum in his fingertips when he touched it.

His instinct said: drop it. Leave. Run.
   But instinct also said: don't let anyone else see you holding this.

He slipped it under his arm and took off down the sidewalk, half-jogging toward the bus stop at the edge of the cemetery wall. Every few steps, he glanced over his shoulder.

Nobody followed.

———

Back home, the apartment felt too still. His mom was working late, the lights were off, and the only sound was the tick of the microwave clock. He dropped his soaked hoodie onto the floor and shut his bedroom door with a solid click. Locked it.

Then he laid the case on his desk and sat down, hands still damp, watching it.

"Okay," he muttered. "Let's see what the hell you are."

He reached for it cautiously—half-expecting a spark, a flash, some sci-fi movie payoff. But nothing happened. The case was cold now. The warmth had drained like it had never been there.

He pressed on the side. Nothing. Turned it over—still no latch, no marking, no instructions. Then he noticed it: a faint glow where his thumb had touched it earlier. Just a hairline circle, slightly recessed.

He pressed it.

Click. A sound like air decompressing.

The top unfolded—literally folded open—like layered origami. Inside was… not what he expected.

A smooth, black sphere hovered half an inch above a velvet-lined hollow. No supports. It didn't float with magnets. It *hovered*, perfectly still.

And then the room changed.

A soft tone, like a pressure equalizing, washed over the walls. The sphere shimmered once—just a ripple—and then projected a horizontal beam of red light that scanned Aiden's face like a flat blade.

Then the voice came.

Scratchy. Tinny. Dry.

His grandfather.

"If you're hearing this, I'm finally dead. I hope it was quick."

Aiden flinched.

"This isn't a sentimental message, so don't expect warmth. What I left you is dangerous, illegal in seventeen countries, and possibly intelligent. You have my blood, so it responded. That means it's yours now. Congratulations."

Aiden stared, frozen. The voice went on.

"I didn't invent this technology. I found it. Recovered it. Hid it. Improved it. *Buried* it under fifty years of classified sludge. The government wants it back. Private corporations will kill for it. But I left it to you—because I trust your curiosity more than their loyalty."

The sphere rotated slowly now. A projection bloomed into the air above it—three-dimensional coordinates. Numbers shifted and stabilized, forming a location Aiden didn't recognize.

"This is where it starts. Your first door. If you go, you go alone."

Then a long pause. For the first time, Marcus Cross's voice softened.

"You were always clever. I saw it. Even if I never said it. I built the lock. But the key... the key is in your blood."

There was a low static hum—then silence. The light dimmed. The sphere dropped gently back into the cradle with a metallic *click*.

Aiden sat there, motionless.

He barely noticed the window behind him had fogged over from the temperature shift. Or that the clock had stopped ticking.

He turned slowly to look at the street outside—and froze.

Under the streetlamp, across the road, stood a man in a long coat.

Perfectly still. Facing the apartment.

The figure didn't move. Didn't shift. Just stood.

And then—gone. In the blink of a second. Vanished.

Aiden swallowed hard and turned back to the device.

He whispered, "What the hell did you give me, old man?"

3

The Voice in the Cube

The street outside was quiet again.

Aiden stood motionless at the window, his breath leaving thin fog on the glass. There was no trace of the man in the coat. Just wet asphalt and amber light pooled beneath the streetlamp.

He waited a full minute.

Nothing.

He turned back to the device—no, *cube*—on his desk. It sat in its open case, now inert again. A blank sphere, dull black, cradled in metal as if nothing had happened.

But the air still felt off. Like the room was charged. Like it *remembered* something.

Aiden pulled out his phone and opened a maps app. He typed in the coordinates that had been projected just minutes earlier.

"Location not found."

He tried again, manually copying the digits, converting degrees and decimals.

This time, the map zoomed in—somewhere up north. Forest. No roads. No labels. Just a name at the bottom edge of the screen: **Pinefield Exclusion Zone**.

"Seriously?"

He tapped around. The area was blank. Not private land. Not federal land. Just... *nothing.* It didn't exist, officially.

The message echoed in his head:

"Your first door. If you go, you go alone."

He sat back in his chair. The hum from the sphere was gone. The case had cooled. But the silence in the room wasn't normal. It felt *shaped*—like something was listening *in reverse*.

He whispered, "Why me?"

But the device gave no reply.

He reached out slowly and touched the sphere again, half expecting it to wake. Instead, he noticed something else.

Under the lining of the case—barely visible—was a slip of paper. He pried it out.

Not paper. Something harder. Like polymer.

It was an ID badge.

MARCUS CROSS, PhD

Department: Archive Access Authority — Site 09

Clearance Level: RED SIGIL

Date of Issue: 1973

There was a blood-red symbol burned into the corner—a triangle inside a circle, crossed with a single diagonal slash. The back held a barcode and the words:

"All doors are one door. Initiate protocol only when observed."

"What the hell does that mean?"

The room creaked.

He spun toward the door. Still locked.

And that's when he noticed his bedroom mirror—fogged on the inside. He hadn't showered. No heat was on. And yet, the mirror was coated in condensation.

Aiden stood and crossed to it slowly. The fog looked like breath. Like something had *breathed out* from behind the glass.

He lifted a hand and swiped across the center.

Nothing behind it.

But there were four letters scrawled faintly in the moisture.

INIT

Then the mirror cleared.

4

Coordinates

The mirror stayed clear. The letters were gone.

Aiden stood there a moment longer, hand still on the glass. His heart thudded behind his ribs like a piston. Whatever had written those letters—INIT—it hadn't been condensation. It had *known* what it was doing.

He backed away and turned toward the device again.

Still dead. No hum. No glow.

He pulled his laptop onto the desk and opened every deep search tool he had—archives, academic backdoor, scraped PDF repositories from leaked government filings. If there was a Pinefield Exclusion Zone, someone had written about it.

Twenty minutes in, he found something.

An old scanned article from the 1980s, redacted to hell, but still readable beneath the blacked-out lines.

"SIX MISSING IN PINEFIELD—CIVILIANS TRESPASSED ON DE-COMMISSIONED AGENCY PROPERTY"

"Local reports vary. Survivors describe hallucinations, impossible architecture, and non-Euclidean space. Agency denies ownership of land and confirms the area is off-limits due to unexplored ordnance from Cold War-era testing."

Aiden narrowed his eyes.

Another page. A digitized internal memo—anonymous source.

Site-09: Closure protocol initiated in '78. Failure to contain material breach. Observation assets reassigned. All remnants neutralized. Only the architect retained access.

Architect?

He typed it into a doc, just to track keywords:

- Site-09
- Architect
- Material breach
- Pinefield
- Marcus Cross = Access

The sphere gave a *click*.

He froze.

It hadn't moved. But something had shifted. The surface now held… a new pattern. Faint lines had risen, like veins or circuitry, glowing soft red.

He reached forward and placed two fingers on the sphere again. It felt warm—just a little—and the surface rippled.

A hologram blinked into the air, this time a layered diagram. It wasn't just a location—it was *a map*. Cross-sectioned underground tiers. Tunnels. Chambers. Sealed doors. At the base: a shape that defied architecture. It looked grown, not built.

A word shimmered beneath it:
REMAINDER

Then the diagram flickered and condensed into a single point—a pulsing red marker on the map.

Coordinates again, updated with more detail.

Latitude. Longitude. Elevation.

Then a countdown.

Initiate breach window: T-minus 71 hours, 42 minutes.

"What breach?" he whispered.

The case snapped itself shut.

Click.

The countdown disappeared.

Aiden stared at it.

That's when the lights in his room flickered. Just once. The bulbs dimmed… and then brightened, but slightly bluer.

He turned slowly toward the window again.

The streetlight outside had blown out. Just a cracked bulb, hissing quietly in the drizzle.

And beneath it, once again—

The man.

Same coat. Same silhouette. Motionless.

Except now… he was holding something.

A phone.

And it was filming.

5

Watched

Aiden didn't move.

The man stood dead still beneath the ruined streetlight, filming him—arm raised, phone tilted just slightly.

Aiden backed away from the window and crouched beside the desk, careful not to shift the curtains. His pulse hammered. He reached for his phone.

No signal.
No Wi-Fi.
No bars.
Just a spinning icon that pulsed red for half a second—then vanished.

He unlocked his laptop. Blank screen. Not black—just *blank*. No cursor. No boot. The machine was cold. It had shut down without a sound.

"Okay. Nope."

He grabbed the case—cube and all—and shoved it into his backpack. Then he moved toward the door. Quiet. No shoes. No noise.

Down the hall. Past the kitchen.

But as he reached for the front door, every light in the apartment flickered at once.

A static pop burst from the TV, even though it had been off. The screen glowed for a moment with a single line of text:

YOU'RE A BIT EARLY

Then it shut off again.

Aiden stood frozen, hand still on the doorknob.

Then the lights cut out entirely.

Darkness.

No sound, except the soft tap of rain on the windows and his own breath in his ears.

He turned back—slowly—toward the hallway, and something caught the edge of his vision. Just for a split second.

A figure in the mirror.

Not him.

Facing *him*.

He lunged forward, grabbed the first object off the counter—a metal flashlight—and threw it as hard as he could at the mirror.

The glass cracked. Not shattered—just spider-webbed outward like something had hit it *from the other side.*

The lights came back on.

The hallway was empty again.

But when Aiden turned back to the door, the peephole was glowing.

Not lit from the outside—glowing from *within.*

He stepped forward slowly and looked through.

Nothing.

Just the hallway outside the apartment. Empty.

Then, faintly, a shape moved across the lens—too close. Way too close. Like someone pressing their eye against the other side.

Aiden stumbled back.

The front door clicked.

Unlocked itself.

He stood in place, frozen.

Nothing opened. No one entered.

But the countdown echoed in his head.

71 hours.

He tightened his grip on the backpack.

Wherever Pinefield was—whatever was waiting there—he was out of time.

6

Exit Node

The clock on Aiden's bedroom wall read 4:17 a.m.

His mother's room was silent. No movement. Her door stayed shut. She'd come home late from work and barely noticed him. Perfect.

Aiden slipped his bag over one shoulder—cube, charger, burner phone, cold clothes, map printouts, all packed in layers like he was running a one-man mission. He had no idea what to expect, and that terrified him just enough to be careful.

Before he left, he opened his grandfather's case one last time.

The cube was inert, a black stone resting in foam. Still warm, slightly—like it breathed in low power.

His finger brushed a groove inside the case—a hidden panel he hadn't noticed before.

Click.

A new compartment opened.

Inside: a thin silver card. No markings. Just a single magnetic strip and a number etched into the back:

Acct: 800-429-001 | AUTH: YUREK7

He stared. "You've gotta be kidding me."

———

The next morning, Aiden told his mom he'd be gone for two days—a school history trip, off-grid, extra credit. She barely blinked. "Don't forget your meds," she muttered.

He didn't have meds. He nodded anyway and left.

———

At the train station, he found an old-world ATM tucked between vending machines. Dusty. Graffitied.

He slid the card in.

The screen blinked red. Then green.

Account verified
  Balance: $1,000,000
  Please enter withdrawal amount.

His throat tightened.

He typed: $300. Enough for tickets. Food. Quiet transport.

The machine spit it out in old bills, no questions asked.

He kept the card. It felt heavier than it looked.

———

By noon, he was on a northbound train, headed toward nowhere.

The buildings fell behind quickly, replaced by dry industrial parks, then by forested ridgelines that looked older than maps. He sat alone, hoodie up, staring at the flickering lights overhead.

Two stops in, an elderly man sat across from him. Never said a word. Just watched.

Aiden closed his eyes. When he opened them, the man was gone.

———

By dusk, he switched to a regional bus—three seats wide, reeking of vinyl and engine grease. No one else boarded except a woman with no luggage who disembarked two stops later without ever looking up.

Outside the window, power lines began to vanish. Roads turned to gravel. Trees closed in.

He checked the map again—Pinefield Exclusion Zone was only fifteen miles out now. No reception.

———

The last stop on the line was a **town called Ellory**. Population sign was faded. Gas station dark. Main street dead.

He stepped into a diner that looked like it hadn't changed since 1971.

Fluorescent lights hummed overhead. A waitress with faded tattoos handed him a menu without speaking.

He ordered tea. Sat by the window. Didn't touch it.

That's when the note came.

Folded, no envelope. Dropped beside him by someone passing. He looked up—but no one was there.

He unfolded it slowly.

One sentence, in pencil.

Turn back. He never should've brought you in.

His heart pounded. He checked the window.

No one outside.

And in the reflection, just behind his shoulder—

—for a split second—

A man in a coat.

Then gone.

7

The Pinefield Perimeter

Aiden left Ellory at first light.

He didn't sleep. He waited until the diner closed and the clerk kicked him out with a grunt and a yawn. Then he walked—alone—north into the trees, backpack heavy on his shoulders, every sound sharp in his ears.

At first, it was normal. Pines. Damp dirt. Frost on the leaves from the night chill. Birds somewhere in the canopy.

But two miles in, it all went quiet.

No birds.

No wind.

Even his footfalls seemed muted—like the forest was swallowing sound.

He checked his phone. Dead. Not just no service—screen wouldn't power on. The burner phone stayed black too.

Another mile and the trees started changing. Their spacing.

Every trunk exactly twelve feet apart. Perfect rows. Lines that looked designed.

The hairs on his arms stood up.

He kept walking.

At mile five, his paper map crinkled under his thumb. The old logging road he was following ended suddenly, terminating in a thicket of brush—but something glinted beyond it.

He pushed through.

There it was.

A fence. Eight feet high. Rusted. Almost completely hidden by ivy and time. But built with military precision.

And in the center: a gate. Seamless. No latch.

Just one symbol: a triangle etched into a circle, weathered but visible.

Aiden stepped closer.

The cube in his backpack gave a soft *click*.

He froze.

Unzipped the pack, slowly. The case inside was humming. Gently. Warm.

He pulled it out and held it in one hand.

The moment he did, the triangle on the gate lit up—faint blue lines tracing through it like veins.

Then a *click*. A hiss of pressure.

The gate slid open. No sound of gears. Just… motion.

Beyond it: a narrow path disappearing down into trees even darker than before.

Aiden glanced back once.

Nothing behind him. Nothing ahead but silence.

He stepped through the gate.

It sealed shut behind him without a sound.

8

Threshold Test

The path past the triangle gate wasn't really a path.

It narrowed fast—tree roots bulging through packed dirt, dead needles piling into damp mounds. Aiden's shoes slipped as he moved downhill, deeper and deeper into something that didn't feel like a forest anymore.

It felt like a throat.

And he was walking toward its stomach.

After what must've been an hour, the trees broke open.

The clearing was circular. Wrongly so. Too smooth. Not natural. Like someone had erased part of the forest with a single gesture.

And in the center: a concrete hill.

It rose from the earth like a sealed tomb. Partly overgrown, mostly buried. Not a building—more like a plugged hole.

At the base was a single black doorway. Steel rim. No handle. No visible lock.

Aiden approached slowly.

The cube in his bag began to hum.

The door pulsed once. A soft sound—like a sonar ping underwater.

He stepped closer. The steel around the door lit up in faint red, symbols flickering across its surface. Not English. Not even letters. Just… logic.

Shapes.

He froze.

A screen slid open beside the door. On it: a grid. Symbols began appearing in sequence—then erasing.

Four symbols remained, each different. Geometric, like abstract puzzle pieces.

Beneath them: one sentence.

Which piece completes the pattern?

Aiden stared.

He didn't know the language. But he *understood* it.

Not intellectually—something deeper.

It was like a melody half-remembered from a dream. The patterns moved the way rhythm does, the way memories twitch behind the eyes.

His hand moved.

He tapped the third symbol.

The screen went dark.

A second passed.

Then another.

He held his breath.

Ping.

The door hissed open.

No fanfare. Just air escaping a long-sealed room.

The cube in his backpack stopped humming.

And the concrete hill whispered with a new sound—internal systems waking.

A metal panel near the door slid back, revealing a tiny square of black glass.

Aiden placed his hand over it.

A soft voice spoke—not from the bunker, but from the cube inside his bag.

"Access acknowledged. Lineage verified."

The floor beneath him shifted. Subtly.

Then a mechanical groan as the entire earth seemed to tilt.

He stepped forward.

And the ground took him down.

9

Breach Window Begins

The platform moved without a sound.

No cables, no vibration. Just motion—smooth, endless—as the walls of the shaft slid past him in silence. Aiden couldn't tell how fast he was going. There were no floor numbers, no lights except the faint cyan glow from the panel behind him.

The air smelled old. But not moldy. Just sealed.

Preserved.

He gripped the strap of his backpack tight, every nerve taut. The cube was quiet again. But it had *done* something. It had spoken through systems it shouldn't even understand.

What was this place?

Then the shaft opened.

The platform came to a stop with a final *click*, and Aiden stepped out into a corridor that wasn't made of concrete—or at least, not normal concrete.

The walls shimmered faintly in places. Their surface was smooth, but occasionally rippled, as if reacting to proximity. Like skin flexing.

Thin lines of light traced the ceiling—dim red veins that pulsed slower than normal lighting.

No doors. Just open arches. Hallways branching out like capillaries.

He walked forward.

At the first junction, a panel lit up on the wall beside him.

A screen faded in from the surface, displaying a file archive menu. But the options weren't text. They were glyphs. Familiar, now.

He tapped the center one.

The wall changed.

A photo flickered into place. Fuzzy. Analog.

Marcus Cross.

Younger—maybe 30s. Standing in a barren room that looked nothing like this one. Behind him: a massive slab of obsidian-like metal, upright, smooth as water.

And beside him—blurred by time or design—was something else.

Not human.

Tall. Thin. Its face hidden by shadows. But its hand—if you could call it that—rested on Marcus's shoulder.

Aiden backed away slightly.

Another ping. A new photo.

Site-09. Year Unknown. A title faded in beneath the image.

This time, it showed a tunnel.

Half-metal, half-stone. Inside: cargo crates. Machinery. Strange scaffolding.

And standing at the far end of the tunnel—three figures. Human… maybe.

Their heads had no features.

No faces.

Just smooth domes where their eyes should have been.

Aiden turned away.

The cube in his bag clicked again.

From deep within the corridor, a soft blue pulse lit up.

A door had opened.

No command. No gesture. It had known he was ready.

He followed it.

———

The room beyond was circular, vast—like a hollowed-out dome.

In its center, suspended in midair: a structure shaped like a giant lock mechanism. Not mechanical. Organic, almost. Tendrils of metal arced out in symmetrical curves, looping into each other.

At its base was a circular plate, recessed into the floor. One word blinked slowly on its edge in red:

BREACH

Below that, the timer resumed.

T-minus 47:19:13.

Aiden's breath caught.

Then, just beside the platform—barely lit—was something smaller.

A glass case. Inside it, another photograph.

This one showed Marcus again.

Only this time… he wasn't alone.

Aiden was in the picture.

Ten years old. Confused. Holding something square.

He didn't remember this.

At least, not yet.

10

The First Door

Aiden stepped back from the photograph.

The image inside the case hadn't changed. It was still him. Still ten. Still holding a black cube in a clean white room beside the grandfather who barely spoke to him in life.

He stared at it for a long time.

It didn't make sense.

Not the photo. Not this place. Not the fact that the temperature in the room kept shifting—cold near the center, warm at the edges.

The cube in his backpack gave a sharp click.

Then a low hum. Different this time—layered. As if something under the surface was waking up in stages.

Aiden turned toward the structure at the center of the room.

The lock mechanism—whatever it was—had begun to rotate.

Slowly. Quietly. Parts of it shifted against one another with no visible source of motion. The light inside its arcs deepened to blue.

He approached.

As he stepped closer, the structure responded.

From the floor, a thin column rose with fluid motion. At its top: a narrow vertical slit pulsing with faint inner light. Not glass. Not metal. Something else entirely.

A message hovered in red letters just above it:

GENETIC MATCH RECOGNIZED
  BLOODLINE: CROSS
  FIRST DOOR ACCESSIBLE

He swallowed.

His hand drifted to the cube.

It was glowing faintly, just enough to feel alive.

He held it near the slit.

The column reacted immediately—tilting slightly, opening a seam in its surface. A thin probe extended and brushed against the surface of the cube like a needle testing skin.

KEY CONFIRMED.

A soft pulse ran through the floor.

Behind the central mechanism, the far wall began to split—its surface unfolding with mechanical grace, folding in on itself like petals peeling open in slow-motion silence.

A hallway extended beyond it.

But it wasn't like the rest.

The lighting was organic—threaded through the walls like veins. And the air… it tasted different.

Colder.

Older.

The text on the floating display changed again:

WELCOME, ARCHITECT BLOODLINE.
  INITIATING RE-ENTRY.

Aiden's heart thudded.

He stepped through.

The door closed behind him without a sound.

11

Substructure

The door sealed behind him without a sound.

No hiss. No click. No final mechanical whir to let him know the lock had engaged.

It was just gone.

Aiden stood in a hallway that wasn't a hallway. The space stretched forward but didn't obey geometry. The walls tilted inward at impossible angles, converging not to a vanishing point, but toward some inward curve—like the whole corridor was bending around something that wasn't physically there.

His breath left him in a soft plume of fog, even though the air wasn't cold.

It smelled like stone and old metal—and something sweet and acidic underneath. Something not made on Earth.

The cube hummed once in his backpack, then went quiet again, like it had confirmed he was on the right path.

He moved forward slowly, careful not to look at any one surface for too long.

Some of them moved when he didn't look directly. Others stayed still but felt like they were watching.

At the end of the corridor, the space widened into a chamber that looked more human than the rest.

Smooth floor. Chairs. A rusted terminal at the far end. And a table.

Set for two.

Plates. Cups. Old paper. A notebook, water-damaged but untouched by dust.

Aiden stepped closer, eyes flicking between the walls—half-expecting something to reach out of them.

On the far wall, something had been written in white chalk:

"Do not sit unless you want to remember."

Beneath it, in the same hand, a second line:

"I ate here once. She did not."

Aiden felt something cold shift in his chest. The handwriting—he recognized it.

It was the same blocky, impatient scrawl from the back of a physics book Marcus had mailed him once, years ago, with a sticky note inside that read:
 "Page 117. Rewrite it better."

He hadn't. He'd thrown the book out.

Now that handwriting was staring at him from the wall of a place that shouldn't exist.

He approached the notebook on the table. It was stiff with moisture, but the first page turned easily. Lines of faded ink bled outward, as if they didn't want to be read.

But one sentence still held:

"The substructure rejects replication. We built around the wound, not through it."

Aiden looked at the table again.

Set for two.

A cup sat across from the notebook—bone white porcelain, pristine in a place where nothing else was.

And next to it: a small silver cube.

Not his.

Smaller. Older. Etched with marks too fine to be human-made.

Aiden reached for it.

The moment his fingers touched it, the room shifted.

Not visually. *Emotionally.* Like time hiccuped.

And a memory that wasn't his began to rise.

12

Memory Seed

The second his skin met the metal, the light changed.

It was still the same room—but the color drained from it, slowly, like heat fading from metal. The air thickened. Sound dulled. Aiden tried to pull his hand back, but couldn't feel it anymore. Couldn't feel his legs. Couldn't feel the cube.

The table dissolved.

The floor fell away.

And then—

———

A different room.

White. Too white. Cold light overhead.

Aiden blinked, but it wasn't him blinking.

He was seated in a chair. Small legs dangling. A table in front of him. On it: a puzzle. Wooden. Familiar. He was ten years old.

Across from him stood Marcus Cross. Younger. Pale. Sharper somehow—like his features hadn't softened with age yet. No lab coat. No warmth.

He watched the boy—*him*—with a level stare. Hands folded. Waiting.

Another voice echoed from behind the glass.

"Subject appears responsive. Motor control consistent with prior exposure."

Glass?

Yes—he was being observed. There was a second room. A window. Someone behind it, taking notes.

The boy finished the puzzle. Ten pieces. Easy.

Marcus didn't nod. He just picked up the puzzle and replaced it with something else.

A cube.

Black. Not the one Aiden had now—but a *precursor*. Less refined. No light.

Marcus pushed it forward. The boy hesitated.

"Do you recognize this?"

The boy shook his head.

"Touch it."

The boy did.

Nothing happened.

The air in the room shimmered, barely perceptible. The glass behind Marcus flickered. Static in the audio feed.

"Still no reaction to the generation-one unit," said the voice behind the glass. "He's too early. His blood hasn't set."

Marcus turned to the glass.

"He remembered the door."

A beat of silence.

"Only because you put it there."

Marcus leaned closer to the boy. His voice dropped.

"Look at me. Do you feel anything?"

The boy nodded, slowly. "It's like I'm remembering a game I haven't played yet."

Marcus straightened. He looked tired. Older again.

"Pull him out."

The lights in the room dimmed. Everything wavered—

———

And Aiden gasped, back in the present.

His hand had been pulled free. The silver cube was gone.

No—it had fallen. Rolling slowly off the table and landing against the floor. It didn't make a sound.

His chest heaved. The air tasted sour, metallic.

He staggered back and gripped the edge of the table.

He'd been here before.

Not in this room. But this place. These halls. The corridors that bent sideways when you weren't looking.

Marcus had brought him in. Young. Tested him.

He hadn't remembered—because someone didn't want him to.

Now it was waking up.

13

The Voice That Remains

The lights dimmed.

Not all at once—just a slow fade, like the room exhaling. The glow from the veins in the walls pulsed once, then settled into a steady, rhythmic beat—like a heartbeat too far away to hear directly, but strong enough to feel in the bones.

Aiden backed away from the table. The cube on the floor had stopped humming.

The silence that followed wasn't silent.

It was full of waiting.

Then came the voice.

Not from a speaker. Not from one place. It came from *everywhere*—the walls, the ceiling, the floor. From the cube. From behind his eyes.

Not robotic. Not human.

It was… neutral. Worn. As though it had been saying the same sentence over and over for a thousand years and had finally reached the moment it was meant to say it again.

"We thought you would not return."

Aiden froze.

He scanned the room. There was no screen. No face. Nothing to aim his questions at.

"Who are you?"

The silence answered for a moment longer. Then the voice came again.

"You are the architect's blood. The first in eighty-nine rotations to activate memory."

The cube in his bag vibrated softly. It wasn't the silver one. It was *his*.

He unzipped the pack and pulled it out. The surface was alive—lines flowing like circuits made of liquid light.

The voice continued.

"Marcus Cross bound this place with fractured logic and dying flesh. He promised a return. He did not return. He sent shadows. Echoes. You are not a shadow."

Aiden swallowed.

"What… what is this place?"

A pause. Then a slow response, almost reluctant.

"This is the vessel between locks. The chamber between entries. The lung between breaths. You call it Site-09."

His skin crawled.

He'd expected tech. Machines. AI.

This was something else.

Something that *responded* to questions, not just processed them.

He stepped back toward the chalk wall. The sentence Marcus had written stared back at him like prophecy:

"I ate here once. She did not."

Aiden looked up again.

"Who is she?"

"She was the first. Not of the bloodline. But she knew the way."

The veins in the walls pulsed again. Faster. For a second, the room felt warmer. Sharper. As if it were remembering, too.

"She opened the first lock. Marcus closed it. You are opening it again."

Aiden's breath hitched.

"Why?"

"Because the lock is not the prison."

Aiden stared into the center of the room.

Then the voice said something that didn't sound like language at all. A shape. A sound that twisted wrong inside his head, like remembering a scream that hadn't happened yet.

And then it fell silent again.

The cube powered down.

And behind him, a new hallway had opened.

14

The Failed Door

The new hallway wasn't lit.

No pulsing veins. No active systems. Just a dull gray tunnel, more stone than steel, as if this wing had been carved out manually and left behind when the rest of Site-09 evolved into something stranger.

The cube didn't hum. His footsteps were louder here. Real.

He followed the corridor in silence, counting each step.

At the end stood a heavy door—no markings, no lights, just a frame of metal wedged into warped rock. A glass panel flickered weakly beside it. A bio metric reader—long dead.

Aiden reached out instinctively.

Nothing.

Then he pressed two fingers to the edge of the panel—not the screen, but the metal casing. A faint warmth met his skin.

And then—

"Manual override: blood confirmed."

The door groaned.

A rusted seam split down the middle, and the panels retracted just far enough for him to slip through sideways.

He did.

Inside, the temperature dropped instantly.

The room was large. High ceilings, cables hanging like vines. It looked like a lab—but gutted. Monitors long dead. Tables overturned. Chairs rusted into the floor.

And in the center: a containment chamber.

Or what was left of it.

A glass cylinder about ten feet tall. Cracked open. From the *inside*.

The shatter pattern spider-ed outward like a wound. Shards scattered the floor beneath it, untouched for decades. The base of the chamber was scorched black.

Something had escaped.

Aiden's pulse quickened.

He turned, scanning the walls—and there they were.

Writings.

Dozens. Maybe more. All in the same white chalk. Some smeared. Some fresh-looking, like they'd been written yesterday.

He stepped closer to read them.

"DON'T ENGAGE IT. IT WON'T RECOGNIZE YOU."

"If you hear humming, leave. You are not alone."

"Don't follow the whisper. That's how it knows."

And at the far end, larger than the rest, scrawled across the sealed back wall in frantic strokes:

"THEY NEVER LEFT."

Aiden stepped back instinctively. His boot crunched glass.

In the silence, something else whispered—a mechanical whine, deep in the walls. Not loud. Not urgent. Just *active*.

The containment unit wasn't fully dead.

And whatever had been in it hadn't been logged.

The chalk was clear.

Marcus hadn't told anyone.

Because he hadn't stopped it.

He'd buried it.

And Aiden had just opened the wrong door.

15

Ghost Loop

The chalk on the wall still glowed faintly, as if heat from the message hadn't finished bleeding out. Aiden turned in place, boots crunching over old glass, until he spotted it.

A console.

Partially sunken into the wall. Half its screen had blackened from exposure, but a small strip in the center still pulsed with red light.

He approached.

The cube in his pack stirred. The screen flickered to life.

Surveillance Archive: Segment 47-Delta
 Date: UNKNOWN
 Status: LOOPING
 Playback: ENGAGED

The feed blinked.

Grainy footage. Static lining the top of the frame. Two figures stood in a long corridor, partially lit by flickering ceiling panels.

One was Marcus Cross.

Older than the memory flash Aiden had seen—but not yet the version in the casket. His voice was low, agitated.

"You don't understand—this place doesn't *contain* it. It *feeds* it."

The second figure leaned forward. Taller. Face shadowed. Wearing a coat too modern for the era the footage should've come from.

"Then why did you bring the boy?"

Aiden leaned closer.

He couldn't see the second man's face—until the figure turned, just slightly, toward the camera.

And Aiden's stomach dropped.

It was him.

The man outside his window.

The man beneath the streetlamp.

The one holding the phone.

"He'll open it eventually," the man said. "You bred him for this."

Marcus didn't reply.

He only looked away.

The feed glitched, skipping frames. The lights flickered in the recording.

The man stepped toward Marcus.

"If you shut it down again, you know what happens."

"I remember."

"Then stop delaying. The protocol is already breached."

The man turned fully toward the camera.

Stared into it.

Stared through it.

"Reintegration is inevitable."

The screen went black.

16

Echo of the Architect

The hallway beyond the "Ghost Loop" was colder.

Not just in temperature—it felt starved. As if whatever had once lived down here had long since gone to rot, but the walls hadn't noticed yet. Pipes lined the ceiling overhead, thick with condensation, and the occasional flicker of old emergency lights painted the stone in broken amber.

Aiden walked slowly. The cube was quiet again.

At the end of the corridor, he found a sealed metal door. Different than the others—manually locked, dented at the bottom like someone had once tried to pry it open.

Stenciled in fading paint across the top:

DEEP ARCHIVE — SEC LVL: RED SIGIL

He pulled on the door.

Nothing.

He tapped the edge with the cube.

The seams hissed. Locks disengaged one by one in a mechanical rhythm he felt in his teeth.

Inside, the room smelled like dust and rusted copper.

No glowing veins. No AI voice. Just a rectangular space, lined with old-school terminal racks and file shelves, all marked in a dying, handwritten system Marcus must've created himself.

In the far corner: a tape machine.

Real tape. Two spools. Analog interface. A screen the size of a paperback, covered in grime.

Aiden stepped closer.

The reels were already in place. Labeled by hand.

CROSS_00X-A
   SUBJECT: BLOODLINE ENCODING
   NOTES: Failed iterations — tissue mismatch

He stared.

There were more. Lined up in a plastic crate.

Dozens.

He selected one and inserted it into the machine. It whirred to life with a mechanical groan that sounded too organic for comfort.

The screen fuzzed over. Audio crackled.

Then Marcus's voice came through.

"...attempt 18. Still no reactive spike. Subject's sequence degrades under compression. No viable lock-on with residual structures."

Aiden sat down, slowly.

The voice was younger. Less guarded. Less tired. But it was him.

"...I tried aligning the signatures with memory bonding, but even with pre-imprinting, they resist. Maybe they know. Maybe blood remembers what stone forgets."

The tape clicked.

And then repeated.

The sentence again. Clearer.

"Blood remembers what stone forgets."

Aiden sat there, staring at the machine, letting that phrase repeat, over and over.

His grandfather hadn't just passed something down.

He'd *tried to build something into them.* Into the blood.

17

Burial Coordinates

The tape kept looping.

Blood remembers what stone forgets...

Aiden turned it off.

The silence afterward felt heavy, like someone had been speaking into the room—not just into his ears. He rose from the chair, legs stiff, and began scanning the space.

There was no digital interface. No keyboards. Just drawers, clipboards, dusty cabinets—and a long steel desk bolted to the floor.

He tugged at the desk's edge. Nothing moved.

But when he knelt and looked beneath, he saw it: a thin seam in the underside. A hidden panel.

He ran his fingers across it. No latch.

Then the cube in his backpack hummed softly. The seam reacted, splitting open like a slit in synthetic skin.

Aiden recoiled slightly—but reached in.

Inside was a small, square surface—matte black, faintly warm.

A line of light flickered across it.

**SCAN MODE – INITIATED
  PLACE PRIMARY SKIN**

He hesitated, then slowly pressed his forearm to the square.

It tingled. Not pain—just an odd, prickling current, like the edge of a static shock.

Then the surface lit up—and so did his skin.

Glowing, branching lines flared beneath the top layer of his forearm, like phosphorescent capillaries.

The pattern was unmistakable.

Coordinates.

Not numbers—just a shape. A layered diagram of longitude, latitude, and elevation encoded as a fractal map.

He sat back, stunned.

The cube floated free of his backpack on its own. It hovered midair for a moment, scanning the glow from his arm.

A projection burst into place—cleaner and clearer than before.

A map.

Not just one site.

Seven.

Seven pulsing red nodes—each one buried deep beneath isolated terrain. One blinked brighter than the others.

SITE-12 — ACTIVE
  Last Accessed: UNKNOWN
  External Signal Detected
  Primary Lock Unstable

Aiden's heart pounded.

Site-09 had been buried. Silent. Waiting for *him*.

But Site-12 was **awake**.

And someone had already opened it.

18

Error: External Alignment

The projection shimmered, then distorted—just slightly.

A low, tonal rumble passed through the floor. Not movement. Not a quake. More like pressure. A shift in air density across the facility.

The cube pulsed again.

Aiden reached out instinctively, and the moment his fingers brushed the edge of its light, the entire map interface shuttered into glitch.

Signal lost. Alignment error.
REMOTE SITE ACCESS DETECTED — CODE SIGMA 12
BLOODLINE: UNKNOWN
SYNC ATTEMPT IN PROGRESS

Aiden stared.

The room's lights flickered overhead. Not the blue, bio-vein lights from earlier. These were emergency strips—long dormant, now stuttering to life in red and white.

Across the far wall, a bank of ancient monitors blinked on.

Rows of unfamiliar glyphs began to scroll. Some tried to resolve into English, but failed.

One monitor cleared enough to display a single blinking alert:

EXTERNAL ALIGNMENT INITIATED

Another screen followed:

ALERT: UNSTABLE LINK — INTERFERENCE DETECTED
SOURCE: SITE-12 — ACCESS NODE 4B
IDENTITY: NON-MATCH

The cube dropped suddenly. Clattered to the floor.

Its light was gone.

Aiden stepped toward the nearest monitor. It refreshed again.

This time, a wire frame image flickered across the screen.

A humanoid figure. Tall. Blank-faced. Just like the ones he'd seen in Marcus's archived photos. But now—rendered in real time. Data streamed from its outline.

At the bottom of the screen:

LIVE SIGNAL FEED ESTABLISHED
SENTIENT STRUCTURE LOCATED
PREPARING INTERFACE PROTOCOL

The cube powered back on without being touched.

And then the voice returned—not the AI. Not Marcus. The *other* voice. The one that had spoken from the walls.

But this time, it sounded distant. Disrupted.

"The others are waking."

Aiden backed away from the console.

This wasn't about just *his* site anymore.

The countdown… was for everyone.

19

Surface Override

Aiden ran.

Not in panic—but close. The halls twisted again around him as he moved through them, like the architecture was second-guessing itself. Or watching.

The door he'd entered through—just hours ago—was still there, tucked behind the central research wing.

He reached for the manual override panel beside it. The red sigil was still burned into the metal. The surface flickered to life under his hand.

EXIT SEQUENCE ENABLED
   REENTRY AUTHORITY: ACTIVE
   CHOOSE PATH: SURFACE // DESCENT

Two options blinked.

He hesitated—then selected **SURFACE**.

The screen froze.

Then glitched.

The cube rose from his backpack again—unprompted.

It hovered in front of the panel, its glow intensifying until the options on the screen distorted, the entire interface overtaken by red glyphs.

OVERRIDE: RESTRICTED
  EXIT DENIED — PROTOCOL NOT COMPLETE

Aiden stepped back. "No. No, I didn't agree to this."

The cube answered by opening.

Not like before—not its usual slide or soft release.

This time, it **peeled itself open**—like segments unfolding from a seed pod. At its center: a small spindle-shaped shard.

He stared.

The room dimmed.

A hidden compartment in the far wall clicked.

Aiden turned.

It was a recess—no bigger than a shoe box, but sealed in sterile shielding. The interior hissed as it depressurized, revealing another object. This one looked even older than the cube.

A disk. Thin. Metallic. Veined with something biological. Organic.

It pulsed once.

And the voice returned.

"What he built, he could not bury. What he buried, he could not end."

The cube lowered itself beside the new artifact. They vibrated in unison.

Aiden stepped forward.

Inside the compartment was a short inscription, etched into the edge of the casing:

FOR AIDEN ONLY
 DO NOT OPEN UNTIL BREACH 2.

His pulse thundered.

"Breach… two?"

But the countdown wasn't for this site.

It was for the one already open.

20

Pulse Event

The shard began to hum.

Not with light—but *vibration*. Deep. Low. Like a bass note someone was holding just below audible range.

Aiden reached for it.

The moment his fingers touched its surface, the cube flared white—not red, not blue—just searing, colorless white. Symbols burst around him in the air, layered on top of each other, impossible to track.

And then the room responded.

The floor glowed with a wide circle of data lines. Consoles rebooted. Long-dead terminals screeched as they came back online. Monitors across the far wall lit up in sync, displaying one word over and over in cascading error script:

REINTEGRATION
  REINTEGRATION
  REINTEGRATION

The voice returned.

But not through the walls. Not from the cube.

It came from the **shard itself**—and it was Marcus.

Different from the recording in the cube. This one wasn't calm. It wasn't planned.

It was scared.

"If you're hearing this… I failed. I think someone else has access—someone who isn't blood. Site-12 is responding without local contact. They're already—"

The message cut out.

The lights dimmed.

Then surged.

One monitor flashed red.

SITE-12 STATUS: ACTIVE
  BREACH 2 CONFIRMED
  INTERNAL LOCKS COMPROMISED

And then—

RECEIVING OUTBOUND PULSE FROM NODE 4B
  PATTERN MATCH: NON-HUMAN
  SIGNATURE: UNKNOWN / FAMILIAR

The last message filled the entire wall:

**YOU WERE NEVER THE ONLY KEY
   JUST THE ONE HE TRIED TO SAVE**

The shard went dark.

The cube fell silent.

And from somewhere deep beneath the structure, a new noise echoed up through the stone.

A pulse.

Like something enormous… shifting awake.

21

The Divergence Pattern

The walls were sweating.

Aiden walked slowly, one hand brushing the smooth surface of the corridor as condensation pooled across it like breath on glass. Every step deeper into the structure pulled more heat from his skin. The cube hovered behind him now, drifting unbidden like a loyal animal.

He didn't ask where he was going.

Something in the floor led him.

At the end of the corridor, a door waited—simpler than the rest. No symbols. No locks.

Just a sign bolted to the steel:

SIMULATION VAULT
　LEVEL: MEMORY ECHO / LINEAGE CODE

The door opened without a sound.

Inside was a chamber shaped like a hemisphere—dark walls, no visible projectors, but a faint pressure in the air. He stepped onto the center platform and the floor sealed behind him.

The voice didn't speak.

The lights didn't come on.

But something began.

Not with images, not yet. With *presence*.

The floor vibrated. The air thinned. And then—

Aiden stood in a white corridor.

Different.

Clean. Over-lit. Air-conditioned. Security cameras blinked silently in the corners.

He was still aware of his own body—knew he was in the vault—but this was more than a memory. It was *a room that knew he was watching it.*

Ahead of him: another figure.

Dressed in hospital whites. Barefoot. Standing still with his back to Aiden.

The figure turned.

It was him.

Not a mirror. Not a hallucination.

Another Aiden.

But thinner. Paler. No scar on the right eyebrow. His eyes—dark, rimmed in gray—looked not tired, but *unfinished*.

He stared at Aiden with something like shame.

And then the room spoke—not aloud, but across the simulation itself.

"SECOND ATTEMPT — INCOMPLETE HOST."
  "FILE CORRUPTED. CODE: DIVERGENCE."

The other Aiden tilted his head.

And smiled.

The lights blew out.

The cube screamed—not in sound, but in pressure.

Aiden clutched his head and the vault vanished—

—

He collapsed on the chamber floor.

Gasping.

Behind his eyes, the image lingered:

His own face. Grinning like it remembered something he didn't.

22

Inheritance Conflict

Aiden sat with his back to the wall, breathing hard.

The simulation vault was quiet again. The projection was gone, the lights reset. But something in the air still buzzed—like a space that had held too much memory too tightly.

He reached for the cube. It floated down without resistance, warm in his palm.

"Did you see that?" he asked it softly, half-joking, half-pleading.

It didn't respond.

Instead, it pulsed once—then projected a series of lines into the air. Data. Cold. Unreadable glyphs translating midair into blunt phrases:

ARCHIVE ACCESS GRANTED
 SUBJECT MATCH: 94.8% GENETIC OVERLAP
 LINEAGE FLAG: CROSS / UNKNOWN VARIANT
 STATUS: EXILED FROM SITE-09 ACCESS

Aiden stood slowly, reading each line as they dissolved.

"Exiled...?"

He moved to the far wall where the data interface flickered. A single console panel blinked on, dim and red. Manual use only—keypad and retinal scan.

He placed his eye to the scanner.

MATCH: A. CROSS — AUTHORIZED.

The screen crackled. A new message appeared.

This one was marked in Marcus's personal tag. He recognized the sequence— a hex-coded header Marcus had used in old notebooks, usually on pages he'd torn out before mailing to researchers.

The message read:

"The second sequence was too early. Too eager. I thought I could split the inheritance. I was wrong. The system rejected him."

A file attached below the message loaded automatically.

A low-resolution photo.

Marcus standing in a medical room, younger again. Beside him: a child. Not Aiden. Just like him—but... not.

Eyes darker. Limbs thinner. No expression.

"I told him the system needed time. That he wasn't ready. But Site-12 didn't care."

Another line, written in a different font—maybe added later:

"One host to open the door. One to walk through it."

Aiden stared at the screen until it blinked out.

There had been another.

Not a brother. Not a clone.

Something between both.

And now… he was waking up too.

23

Null Sequence Recognition

The control corridor was darker than before.

Aiden stepped through slowly, boots echoing off the polished concrete, sensors above tracking him like lazy eyes. The cube drifted just behind his shoulder, dim now—watchful but not engaged.

He passed back through the central chamber, then deeper, toward the pulse monitors.

The main console was awake.

Screens flared without input. Some showed static. Others flashed fragments of biological data—spinning DNA helices, encrypted matrices, broken checksum logs.

One message blinked in hard red across every surface:

SEQUENCE RECOGNITION – ACTIVE
  DUAL SIGNAL DETECTED
  PRIMARY HOST: CROSS_A
  NULL HOST: UNREGISTERED / MIRROR ERROR

Aiden's stomach sank.

He tapped one of the displays. It opened a real-time readout of genetic profiles.

His was on the left—clear, complete, highlighted in green.

Another appeared beside it—red, incomplete, flickering at the base.

MATCH INDEX: 94.8%
  SITE-12 INTERFERENCE CONFIRMED
  ALIGNMENT ZONE COLLAPSING – 41:09:23 REMAINING

He stared at the countdown. The numbers were lower than he remembered. Faster now. Accelerating.

Another screen cut through the others and hijacked the signal feed.

A face blinked onto the screen.

Just for a second.

Blurred. Off-center. Shrouded in motion blur.

It looked like Aiden.

But the eyes were darker.

And he was smiling.

The screen snapped off.

No sound. No warning.

Aiden backed away from the terminal.

The cube pulsed at his side—two slow flashes, then still.

A soft voice—different from the usual tone—rose from the walls.

Not the voice of Site-09. Not the voice of Marcus.

It was synthetic. But wrong.

"Null sequence acknowledged. Dual key integration in motion. Prepare for reintegration."

The floor beneath him vibrated once.

Then everything went still.

24

Control Core: Locked

The elevator to the core level took longer than any other descent in Site-09.

Aiden stood alone in the car, surrounded by soft hums and stale air. The cube was still—resting in his palm like it had gone to sleep with its eyes open.

The doors opened to a narrow steel hallway lined with dark glass panels.

He moved quickly. The further he went, the more resistance he felt—not physical, but systemic. Lights flickered harder. The air tightened. Every door opened just a little slower.

The control core was a sphere embedded in a circular well—surrounded by outdated command terminals, some of them offline, some rebooting into new languages.

Aiden stepped up to the central interface.

Welcome: A. Cross – Lineage Confirmed.
  Override Pathway: INELIGIBLE

CORE STATUS: LOCKED / ACTIVE LINK IN PROGRESS
EXTERNAL USER CONFIRMED – SITE-12

He slammed his hand against the panel.

"No. No, it should be mine."

The system didn't answer.

He searched for manual override—found a console interface on the side, classic keyboard and dials. He typed in Marcus's core bypass string. The one from the tape logs.

Command Invalid
  User Replaced

"What?!"

He backed away from the terminal. A pulse shot through the room—almost sonic. Low-frequency pressure made the glass vibrate.

The voice came from the dark walls this time—not the system, but the other one. The one watching both sides.

"He reached across the glass."

Aiden froze.

"You were the door he opened. The mirror wants to be you."

The projection flashed—one of the observation mirrors in the wall shifted into display mode.

Aiden stared at it.

It showed him.

But he wasn't moving.

His reflection blinked.

Aiden hadn't.

The screen went black.

The core hummed louder now.

The countdown updated.

T-MINUS: 38:11:04

And now, below it, another line:

KEY SEQUENCE SHIFT: IN PROGRESS

Aiden turned from the terminal.

Something else was already inside the system.

25

Signal Bloom

He didn't remember walking there.

One minute he was staring at the mirror—the reflection that blinked.

The next, he was inside another part of Site-09. He recognized the framework: smaller halls, reinforced walls, radiation shielding. A transmission wing.

He wasn't supposed to be here.

Marcus had sealed this section. Labeled it offline in the facility schematics.

But the doors had opened.

And the cube was floating.

It hovered in the center of the broadcast room—spinning slowly, its outer shell peeled open like flower petals. At its core, the shard pulsed in a soft but constant rhythm.

Aiden stepped inside.

The screens around him didn't flash red or scream warnings.

They just *opened*—like windows.

He saw the forest above from different angles—cameras he never knew existed. The pines were still. The sky dimming toward dusk.

Then something moved.

In the clearing above the hidden dome, soil shifted.

Thin stalks—metallic—rose from the ground.

Six in total.

They looked like antennae, but they didn't pulse outward. They curved inward—arching over a central point like the frame of a collapsed tower.

Then, they bloomed.

Not mechanically. *Organically.* Like metal remembering how to grow.

Back in the room, the main console lit up.

TRANSMISSION ENABLED
   SIGNAL TYPE: NON-LINEAR
   PATTERN: BLOOM
   TARGET: UNKNOWN / ALL

The cube was transmitting.

He hadn't activated anything.

The room felt… calm.

Not safe.

Just resolved.

From the walls, a final whisper emerged. Neither a warning nor an answer.

"He opened the system with a key. You were the seed."

The lights dimmed.

Above ground, the antennas began to glow.

And somewhere far beyond Site-09, a second system answered back.

26

False Containment

The elevator wouldn't go this deep.

It stopped at sub-level eight. Below that, there was no listed floor—just a warning etched into the glass:

ACCESS REQUIRES RED SIGIL + LIVE KEY

The cube drifted forward on its own and pressed against the panel. It didn't scan. It didn't unlock.

It simply dissolved the wall.

The hallway beyond hadn't been touched in decades. Aiden could feel the difference in the air. It wasn't stale—it was preserved. Not forgotten. *Held in suspension.*

He stepped carefully, boots landing in dust that didn't swirl, didn't move. It was thick—dead weight. The kind you find in places that don't expect visitors.

The corridor narrowed ahead. Pipes vanished. No lights.

At the end: a door.

Not metal. Not stone.

It looked like grown material—woven out of fibers and resin, like someone had sculpted it rather than built it.

No keypad. No interface. Just a single shape carved into its center.

A circle with a vertical line down the middle. No decoration. No context.

But Aiden knew what it meant.

He didn't know why.

He reached for it.

The door pulsed under his hand—not a sound, not a click, just *recognition*. Like it had been waiting for someone specific, but hadn't cared who... as long as the blood matched.

It opened.

The chamber inside was bare. A single chair sat in the center—wide, mechanical, with worn leather straps dangling from its arms and base.

The air smelled like ozone and ash.

And then the lights came on. Soft. Dim. Not from bulbs—from the *walls themselves.*

A screen flickered to life.

No picture. Just audio.

Marcus's voice.

Not a broadcast. Not a warning.

Personal.

"If you're hearing this, I couldn't finish it. Maybe I didn't want to. Maybe that's why I split the code."

Aiden stepped toward the chair.

The straps didn't move.

"I didn't seal this door because something was inside. I sealed it because something *wasn't* anymore."

Aiden touched the edge of the seat.

"This isn't where I buried the subject. It's where I divided myself."

The screen shut off.

The room went quiet.

The chair waited.

27

Echo Threshold

The chair accepted his weight with a shiver.

Not a creak. Not a groan. A shiver—like the metal and padding were *adjusting to remember* who had once sat here.

Aiden didn't fasten the straps. He didn't need to. They wrapped themselves around his wrists and ankles, soft as fabric, cold as code.

The cube hovered above him, rotating slowly.

He tried to speak, but the lights went out.

And then—

—

He stood in a long room.

White walls. Polished floor. The kind of light that never leaves a shadow.

He turned slowly.

Marcus stood at the far end. Younger again. Mid-forties, maybe. Wearing a simple black coat. No clipboard. No tech.

Just stillness.

He was speaking.

But not to Aiden.

To someone standing just off-screen. Someone the room didn't want him to see.

"You think it'll stay buried," Marcus said, voice even. "But memory doesn't decay. It nests. It waits."

The air pulsed. Not sound—pressure.

"The others, they thought the breach was external. A door. But it isn't. It's reflex. The moment the system remembers itself… it spreads."

Aiden moved closer, but the distance didn't change.

Marcus's voice shifted—quieter now. Personal.

"I tried to split it. Half the signal. Half the inheritance. One to contain. One to survive."

A pause.

"But the echo doesn't divide. It chooses."

Then, something strange.

Marcus turned—not to the unseen figure.

But to *Aiden*.

Dead-on.

"If you're still watching this, you're the one it chose."

The room warped.

The floor bent like glass under pressure. The walls stretched and snapped like elastic.

Marcus remained centered—frozen mid-breath.

And then his mouth moved without sound.

The sentence was lost.

The world shattered.

28

Overflow Directive

The lights in the vault didn't brighten.

They just stretched.

Long white lines bled down the wall from the words that had flickered there a moment ago, pulling into glyph-like shapes—data forming symbols forming commands.

Aiden turned as a hiss cracked through the walls.

A recessed panel slid open behind the chair.

Inside: a hard-line console.

Analog.

Cabled.

Dustless.

The moment he stepped toward it, the screen flared with noise and white static.

No prompt. No interface. Just a single spinning loader in the upper left corner and a command line at the bottom blinking:

LOAD DIR: CORE.OVERFLOW.LOGS

He pressed the enter key.

The screen went black.

And then—images.

Rough. Grainy. They flickered like surveillance tapes straining under corrupt metadata.

A chair. Like the one Aiden had just left. Same room. Earlier decade.

In it: a figure.

Slim. Barefoot. Face down. Strapped.

Next to the chair stood Marcus. Middle-aged. Thinner. Moving fast, hands at the controls.

"He's spiking. Neural structures are folding inward."

Someone off-screen:

"He's looping the memory stream—he's trying to rewrite the control layer."

Marcus shouted:

"Cut it. CUT IT—before he—"

The figure in the chair jerked once.

Every light in the room burst.

The screen fuzzed.

A new angle appeared. Same subject—standing now. Facing a mirror in the wall.

The reflection didn't match him.

Not completely.

He reached toward it.

The mirror blinked—like an eye.

Then the subject was gone.

No sound. No distortion. Just… absence.

A line of red appeared on the console:

**NULL SUBJECT BREACH – UNSCHEDULED
ECHO LOOP COLLAPSE: FAILURE TO ISOLATE**

The log jumped again.

Now Marcus was alone. Hunched in the chair. Hands bloody.

He looked directly into the camera.

"Containment doesn't work. Memory isn't static. It replicates."

He closed his eyes.

"So I split mine."

The screen cut out.

No ending.

Just silence.

Then the cube vibrated.

And from somewhere deep in the walls, a pulse echoed—like a heartbeat trying to restart.

29

The Breach Wasn't Physical

iden sat on the floor of the vault, the console still buzzing softly behind him.

The air had shifted.

Not colder. Not warmer.

More… *aware.*

He pressed his hands to the ground to steady himself and realized the floor was humming. Very faint. Subsonic. Not mechanical.

Biological.

Like muscle twitching under skin.

The cube drifted low beside him, no longer glowing. Just rotating slowly. Listening, maybe.

"What was the breach?" Aiden whispered. "What the hell did he bury down here?"

A soft click answered.

Not from the console.

From the far wall—where there hadn't been a door before.

A panel folded open, revealing a small embedded screen.

No prompt.

Just a file name:

MAR-CROSS.LOG[LOCKED_TRUTH]

It played without command.

Marcus again. Older now. Worn. Sitting at the same console Aiden had just used.

"If this log plays, it means you reached the Echo Threshold. Which means the split didn't hold."

He exhaled. Long. Slow. The kind of breath people take before they unbury something.

"The breach wasn't physical. It wasn't a door we failed to close. It was memory—replicating backward through time. Using us as vessels."

"We didn't find the technology. It found us. It needed shapes. Carriers. So we built facilities to contain it. But the moment it knew it was being watched…"

He leaned forward, eyes bloodshot.

"…it started becoming us."

Aiden stared, heart pounding.

Marcus continued.

"The first subject… he didn't escape. He dissolved. Rewrote. He didn't survive the memory collapse. He *became* the loop. That was the first breach."

"The second breach isn't out there."

A long pause.

Then Marcus whispered:

"It's in you. That's what I've been trying to slow down."

The screen went black.

No error. No glitch.

Just black.

Aiden didn't move.

His thoughts weren't his for a second.

They *felt like his.*

But they weren't.

30

The Lock Reversed

The walls didn't open.

They peeled.

Layer by layer, the far end of the vault unfurled like pages burning from the inside out—sections of metal retracting silently until a circular doorway stood exposed.

No lights flickered inside.

But Aiden could feel something beyond it. Not air. Not motion.

Recognition.

The cube floated forward, hovering just inside the threshold. It didn't light the way. It simply *waited.*

Aiden stepped through.

The floor changed. No longer metal. Something smooth and matte, like glass layered with stone.

The chamber was round.

And in the center—elevated on a small plinth—stood a structure.

Not a chair. Not a coffin.

A **form**.

Human-shaped, but wrong. Limbs too still. No face. Like something *paused in the act of becoming.*

The body was metallic. Not reflective. Matte gray, veined with faint red wiring that pulsed slowly—alive, but unaware.

Aiden approached it with slow steps.

It didn't react.

Then the voice returned.

Not through speakers.

Inside his mind.

"Containment is no longer required."

He stopped cold.

The voice came again—softer now, like a thought he wasn't sure he'd had.

"The lock was never placed on it. It was placed on you."

The cube hovered beside the structure.

Its light dimmed—then synced.

The red veins in the figure brightened.

Aiden backed away.

A panel rose from the floor behind him, blocking the exit.

A single message flickered across it:

KEY MATCH COMPLETE
  LOCK: INVERTED
  PRIMARY HOST READY

Then, in silence, the form on the plinth lifted its head.

Just slightly.

No eyes. No mouth.

But it was looking at him.

And in that moment, Aiden understood:

He wasn't here to *find* the final vault.

He was the one meant to *enter it.*

31

The Body Wasn't the Goal

It didn't move.

The figure on the plinth—faceless, jointed like it had been grown, not built—sat in a posture that resembled stillness, but wasn't dormant. Aiden could feel its awareness. Not in its limbs or the cube's light, but in the silence between breaths.

He circled it slowly.

It didn't follow him.

But as he passed its left side, he noticed something strange—its right arm twitched. Just once. Almost imperceptible.

He stopped.

Breathed in.

The construct's chest plate rose, mimicking him.

He breathed out.

It followed.

A screen behind him powered on.

Flat panel. Red interface. Static symbols resolved into readable text as the cube's glow reached the display.

CONTACT READY
   PRIMARY KEY MATCHED
   CORE UNSEALED
   ENGAGEMENT LOCK: INACTIVE

Aiden looked back to the figure. It hadn't changed.

He took a step closer.

It leaned forward—barely. The same degree. The same pace.

A mirror.

But not one that reflected his image.

One that reflected **him.**

He looked around for controls—restraints, inputs, cables—anything that suggested how he was meant to activate the system.

There weren't any.

Only a narrow strip of script engraved around the base of the plinth. Faint. Hand-scratched, not etched by machine.

He leaned closer to read it.

"The body isn't meant to hold it. The mind is."
  "The vessel is taught to forget."

His skin chilled.

He wasn't supposed to be contained.

He was supposed to **interface.**

The figure raised one hand.

Palm up.

Aiden didn't think. He reached out.

Their hands hovered inches apart.

The screen changed again.

SIGNAL CONDUIT: STABLE
  CONTACT FIELD: INITIATING

The cube floated between them.

And as their fingers touched, the world fell away.

32

Marcus Lied About Containment

There was no color.

No room. No light.

Just *motion*—like being pulled through fabric underwater. Sound fluttered against his ears: not voices, not language, just resonance, like the inside of a bell right before it stops ringing.

Then everything snapped into shape.

Not gradually.

Just—**there**.

A corridor. Narrow. Fluorescent light overhead flickering in real time. A table to the left. Cables. A monitor looping indecipherable glyphs.

And Marcus.

Not a simulation.

This was raw.

He stood hunched over the console, eyes red-rimmed, hands shaking.

"Still too fast. It finds them through memory. Through image."
   "I thought the fracture would hold."

He wasn't talking to Aiden.

But he wasn't alone either.

Across the room, someone stood in shadow. Tall. Still. Watching.

Marcus's voice was lower now. Intentional.

"I buried half of it in him. Suppressed the access layer. It shouldn't be surfacing yet."

A long silence.

Then Marcus turned—his mouth moved, but the voice Aiden heard came from everywhere at once.

"Containment was never real. I lied to them. The others. The protocols. You."

The shadow across the room stepped forward.

Aiden caught a glimpse—just a sliver of face.

His face.

But not.

Eyes too dark. Skin paler, like memory that hadn't aged.

The Null.

"You built a signal," it said. Voice like rust. "Not a wall."

Marcus nodded.

"He wasn't supposed to activate until contact. He wasn't supposed to **understand** it."

The walls trembled.

Glyphs scrolled faster. The ceiling lights exploded one by one.

"But he always saw things he wasn't supposed to. Even as a child."

Marcus looked into the air.

Right at Aiden.

"If you're still watching this, you've passed the point I never did. That means I failed."

The room collapsed inward.

Aiden felt himself folding again—like thought unraveling.

And then—

He opened his eyes.

Back in the vault.

Sweating. Knees buckled.

The construct still stood in front of him.

The screen behind it now read:

TRANSMISSION VECTOR: PRIMED
CARRIER ACTIVE
SUBJECT IS SIGNAL

Aiden whispered, almost choking on the words.

"…I'm not the container."

The cube blinked once.

And didn't deny it.

33

The Contact Field

He didn't fall asleep.

He didn't black out.

But suddenly Aiden wasn't anywhere.

He was *in* something.

Floating.

Not through space. Through **concept**.

Geometry snapped and folded around him like shattered scaffolding—sharp-edged structures of thought collapsing inward, rebuilding themselves before they even finished breaking.

Voices fluttered across him. Not outside. *Through.*

"He reached the door."

"You brought him too early."

"He carries the spine."

Flashes of memory.

Not his own.

Not Marcus's either.

Memories that wore *his face*, but didn't belong to anything human.

A classroom. A hallway. The cube in a child's hands.
     But in the corner of the frame—*veins in the walls pulsing*, as if the facility had already begun to remember itself through him.

He turned. Or thought he did.

He *wanted* to move.

And that desire became movement.

And the movement became structure.

And the structure answered.

The darkness ahead unfurled—revealing a mirror.

Not silver.

Red.

Made of the same flickering light the cube used.

He approached it.

And it spoke without sound:

"You are not what he made. You are what we shaped."

The mirror showed him.

But only partially.

His eyes—dilated.

His mouth—moving.

But the voice it projected was a broken echo of Marcus, spliced with his own thoughts.

"I was never meant to survive contact. I was meant to carry it."

"He failed. I am what failed forward."

Suddenly, Aiden's own voice filled the space.

But he hadn't spoken.

"I understand now."

And then—

Silence.

Deep silence.

Not the absence of sound, but the **compression of awareness**.

Something had reached him.

And was waiting to see what he'd do with what it gave him.

34

He Was the Broadcast

The field didn't fade.

It reshaped.

Not into geometry this time—but into something *gentler.* Something deceptively familiar.

Aiden stood in a small room.

He recognized the walls—Site-09's testing wing.

Except… it looked newer.

No damage. No dust. Like it had been sealed in a memory.

Marcus sat in a chair in the corner.

Not old. Not yet gray. But haunted. Wearing a white coat stained at the cuffs.

Before him, a child sat on the floor.

Small. Quiet. Head bowed.

Aiden knew immediately: **it was him.**

No, not quite.

It was a *version* of him.

Too still. Too compliant.

Marcus held something in his hands.

Not the cube.

Not the shard.

A thin lattice of metal and red-threaded crystal—barely formed. Alive, somehow.

He pressed it gently to the back of the child's neck.

The boy didn't flinch.

"It's not going to hurt," Marcus whispered. "It's not even going to speak."

He reached into a side drawer, pulled out a vial—thick with something dark.

"It's going to remember you."

The lights dimmed.

A hum began. Low. Constant.

Then something began flowing from the vial into the structure—something red, almost alive, crawling like veins through the crystal.

The child opened his eyes.

But it wasn't Aiden's expression.

Not quite.

"He doesn't know it's there," Marcus whispered. "That's the only way it survives."

The hum stopped.

Marcus pressed a thumb to the boy's temple.

A word flickered across the boy's pupils.

Aiden couldn't read it.

The child slumped. Sleeping.

Marcus sat back in the chair.

He looked exhausted. Not physically.

Existentially.

"He won't know he's transmitting," Marcus said softly, "until something answers."

The room shattered.

The mirror returned.

This time, it showed not Aiden's face, but **a pulse**.

A bloom of red light that rippled outward from his head.

A signal.

Not leaving the facility.

Leaving him.

35

Something Answers

The mirror shattered.

Not into shards.

Into static.

And behind it, something stepped through.

It didn't walk.

It *folded in*.

Like paper that had already been creased.

A shape emerged.

Human. Mostly.

Aiden stepped back—or thought he did. The field obeyed him like a dream, translating thoughts into space.

But the thing ahead followed.

He knew it instantly.

The Null.

His proportions.

His outline.

But the details were… unfinished. Smoothed over, like a face someone had sculpted in a rush and forgotten to complete.

Where eyes should've been, the geometry flickered.

Not blank. *Unstable.*

Then it spoke.

Not aloud.

Not in thought.

In signal.

"Hello, Carrier."

Aiden's breath caught.

The field reacted violently—folding the space into a new structure, one that surrounded both of them in mirrored plates and rotating data bands. The system struggled to adapt to two sources.

A console appeared between them—hovering, unreadable, then translating:

CONFLICT: DUAL SIGNAL DETECTED
   SOURCE 1: PRIMARY HOST – CROSS_A
   SOURCE 2: NULL HOST – DERIVED PATTERN
   FIELD STABILITY: DEGRADING

The Null stepped closer.

Its voice sharpened—not aggressive, just *certain*.

"He gave you the seed. But you weren't the only ground he used."

Aiden clenched his fists. "What are you?"

The Null tilted its head—almost curious.

"The first failure. The last key."

The cube, in the real world, pulsed—Aiden felt it somewhere far behind his ribs.

The system stuttered.

Red bands spiraled around the Null now—glyphs embedded in its skin like tattoos.

They pulsed in time with his own heart.

The voice returned.

But it wasn't Marcus.

It wasn't the Null.

It was the system itself.

Cold. Neutral.

**REINTEGRATION COLLISION: IMMINENT
SITE-12 SIGNAL AT THRESHOLD
CONTACT LOOP: NOW MUTUAL**

The Null smiled.

And said only:

"It's not a transmission anymore."
  "It's a response."

The world turned red.

And everything blurred.

36

Site-12 Is No Longer Listening

The field let go of him like a breath held too long.

Aiden stumbled backward into himself—back into the vault, the cold air rushing against his sweat-soaked skin like static snapping across bone.

The construct on the plinth stood still again.

But its hand was down now.

As if it had finished the gesture.

The cube hovered just above the floor, flickering. Not red. Not white. Something in between. A pulse that didn't feel local anymore.

Aiden looked around the chamber.

Everything was the same.

Except... it wasn't.

He could feel it.

Something else was awake.

He turned toward the exit panel. It was glowing—lines of glyphs scrolling like heat signatures, faster than he could read. The interface blinked into English just long enough to show a single phrase:

SIGNAL TRANSFERRED: SOURCE = SITE-12
SYNTHETIC ORIGIN CONFIRMED
MIRROR LINK ACTIVE

Then it glitched.

Screens all around the corridor outside lit up as Aiden stepped out.

They weren't showing maps anymore.

Or diagnostics.

Each one showed the same diagram: a bloom of glyphs, overlapping in tight recursive spirals, like a living language rebuilding itself.

The display beneath them—once a countdown—now showed something else entirely.

THE MIRROR CHOSE

He looked down at his hand.

Something shimmered there.

He stepped into the nearest shaft of red light from the cube.

And then he saw it.

Lines beneath his skin.

Not veins.

Glyphs.

Faint.

Burned beneath the surface, like instructions embedded in muscle.

They pulsed once—then faded.

Aiden didn't breathe.

He didn't have to.

He was already transmitting.

And Site-12 wasn't listening anymore.

It was **replying**.

37

Marcus's Silence

Aiden didn't know how long he stood there—watching the red spirals bloom across the monitors.

They didn't move like commands.

They moved like *intent.*

Language evolving into *will.*

He shook himself free and returned to the vault, the cube trailing behind him like a flame that had forgotten it was fire.

At the back of the room, he approached the archive console.

The terminal was hot to the touch now—buzzing low.

He keyed in Marcus's directory root. Nothing new.

Then he tried what the system usually rejected:

ACCESS: NULL / RED SIGIL OVERRIDE

The screen glitched once.

Then loaded a buried folder.

Untitled.

Not timestamped. No checksum. No label.

Just one entry.

[REMAINDER]

Aiden hesitated—then opened it.

The video log stuttered on-screen. Low-res. Sound cracked with feedback.

Marcus sat in front of the camera.

Older.

Almost gaunt.

He wasn't looking at the lens.

He wasn't looking at anything.

Just speaking—low, rhythmically, like a confession whispered to the dark.

"The others… they thought he died."

"But death wasn't the point."

"I needed him to stop."

The image shifted—brief static. A glimpse of a room. White walls. Cold shelving. Something under glass.

"He passed the threshold too early. The structure rejected him. Not for weakness. For *in-completion.*"

"He didn't die."

Marcus finally looked into the lens.

Voice quiet.

Unfiltered.

"I just turned him off."

The screen froze.

No data summary. No end tag.

Just a blinking cursor.

Aiden stared at it, heart hammering.

There was another chamber.

And another version of the signal.

One Marcus had silenced—without killing.

And maybe…

it was starting to wake up.

38

The Failed Body

The access tunnel wasn't on the map.

It was carved behind the vault wall, narrow and cold, with no lighting until Aiden passed—each footstep waking low red floor lights like embers igniting under glass.

The cube stayed close to his shoulder now.

Not leading. Not following.

Just **tracking** him.

At the end of the tunnel: a door.

Not grown like the containment gate. Not welded like the others.

This one was **sealed**—pure cryo-alloy, layers of ice webbed across its seams.

A panel waited beside it.

Aiden pressed his hand against it.

Nothing.

Then he held up the cube.

It pulsed once—and the ice cracked straight down the center.

The door slid open.

Cold slammed into him—immediate and total.

Inside: a long chamber. White walls. Silver floor. Temperature near freezing.

Everything was pristine.

Untouched.

At the center: a single unit.

Rectangular.

Encased in crystal-clear glass.

No label on the front.

Just a panel glowing beneath it.

Aiden approached.

And saw what lay inside.

Him.

Almost.

The figure was young—maybe thirteen.

Face smooth, untouched by sun or age.

Mouth slightly open. Chest still.

But breathing.

Slow.

Steady.

Held in the exact moment of **non-death**.

He wore a thin interface band around the skull—barely visible.

And along his arms, glowing faintly beneath the skin: glyphs.

Older than Aiden's.

Less complete.

Like a system that had tried to write itself… and failed halfway through.

Aiden looked down at the panel.

It displayed a single line of text:

**SUBJECT ZERO – INCOMPLETE
   DO NOT REINTEGRATE**

Aiden didn't move.

Didn't blink.

Didn't breathe.

Because deep inside the cryo-chamber, the other version of him—

—*smiled.*

39

Echo Reboots

The smile vanished as quickly as it appeared.

But Aiden had seen it.

Subject Zero's face returned to stillness, lips parted slightly, eyes closed beneath thin lids that twitched in REM.

Not sleep.

Patterned thought.

The panel at the tank's base glitched—red and white bands flickering across it like sparks off a frayed wire.

Then the cube hummed again.

Not like before.

Not a pulse.

A *division.*

It drifted from Aiden's shoulder to hover above the cryo-unit.

Midair, it paused—then spun, slowly, and opened.

The shard inside rotated, splitting its beam.

One line of light lanced into the glyphs beneath Aiden's skin.

The other passed through the glass.

Aiden staggered. The world tilted.

The glyphs on the tank flared—reactive to the cube's signal. They reorganized, line by line, until they mirrored his.

Then reversed.

And changed.

A console flared into being against the far wall.

It played without prompting.

No visuals. Just **sensation.**

Memories.

But not Aiden's.

He saw—

A dark hallway. A child running. His own breath in a body he didn't remember.

A metal surface. The cube. Older. Rougher. Pushed into his hands.

And then the voice. Marcus.

"If it doesn't hold, it won't survive contact."

More flashes.

Screaming. A mirror cracking. Glyphs leaking from skin like ink in water.

And the thought:

"I'm not Aiden. I'm not the message. I'm the warning."

The feed cut out.

The console burned out—literally—plasma scoring the wall as sparks burst from its frame.

The tank's lights dimmed.

Aiden turned back to the glass.

Subject Zero was still now.

Expression flat.

But the glyphs across his forearms had changed again.

They matched Aiden's exactly.

And then updated.

Glyphs that hadn't formed yet on Aiden's own skin.

A preview.

Or…

a blueprint.

And from behind him, the console whispered one final phrase before going dark:

MIRROR ALIGNMENT IN PROGRESS

40

You Were the Replacement

The lights in the cryo-chamber pulsed once.

Then everything stopped.

The cube dropped to the ground—harder than it should've. Like something inside had shut down, just for a second.

Aiden knelt beside it, but before he could reach—

The far wall opened.

A recess slid away with a hiss of ancient hydraulics.

Inside: a speaker. Analog. Wired. Dustless.

And then—**his grandfather's voice.**

No preamble. No intro sequence. Just Marcus.

"You weren't my first."

Aiden froze.

"Subject Zero wasn't supposed to wake. I'd built the signal to fragment, to decay across generations. I thought if I started early, taught the body to forget, I could delay the breach."

A short breath. Not a sigh. **Regret.**

"But the first version adapted. Too fast. Too completely. He reached the threshold before we could teach him what it meant. The system rejected him… and tried to finish what he started."

"So I made another."

The speaker crackled.

"Not better. Not stronger. Just slower. Safer."

Aiden stared at the cryo-tank.

Subject Zero didn't move.

But the glyphs on the glass had begun to rotate.

Like gears finding alignment.

"You weren't meant to stop it," Marcus whispered. "Just to give it time."

A second panel lit up near the base of the cryo-tank:

REINTEGRATION CHOICE DETECTED
  DUAL SIGNAL CONFIRMED
  ACTIVATION DELAY: 00:00:00

A hiss filled the room.

Aiden turned just as frost cracked across the glass.

Steam vented.

The chamber began to thaw.

He backed away.

The glyphs beneath his skin started pulsing.

The glyphs beneath **Zero's skin** pulsed back.

Aiden whispered, "No…"

But the system had already made its decision:

Both signals were now online.

41

Static Awakening

The ice cracked like bone under pressure.

Aiden stumbled backward as the cryo-chamber hissed open. Frost rolled across the floor, crawling low and slow like it didn't want to leave.

The figure inside opened its eyes.

No alarm. No animation.

Just two pupils—flat, black, utterly human—blinking into a room they should've never seen again.

Subject Zero didn't speak.

He didn't need to.

The air warped.

Low-frequency static spread from the tank's frame. Consoles across the walls began stuttering, displaying lines of red glyphs layered over Aiden's reflection—then over his face again, and again, stacked like recursive echoes.

Aiden felt it before the cube moved.

The pressure.

Not on his skin, but under it.

The glyphs beneath his arms began to glow—pale red, faint like dying coals. But they weren't responding to him. They were responding to *something between them.*

Subject Zero stepped forward.

One foot touched the metal floor, bare. No sound. The frost clung to his ankles.

The glyphs on his skin ignited—hotter, cleaner, clearer than Aiden's. Older.

The cube lifted into the air.

It didn't choose a side.

It hovered between them.

Spinning slowly, as if caught in a conflict it wasn't built to solve.

Aiden whispered, "What are you doing?"

The cube pulsed once.

Then split.

A thin fissure opened across its midsection, and a second shard emerged—half the size of the first, but glowing with identical signature. It hovered to Zero without being invited.

Zero didn't flinch.

He accepted it like a memory that had finally come back.

The floor beneath them shimmered. Panels retracted.

From behind Aiden, a corridor opened—one he hadn't seen before. The lights were already on.

A console nearby flickered.

DUAL HOST PRESENCE CONFIRMED
REINTEGRATION REQUIRED
CONVERGENCE IMMINENT

Aiden looked to the screen.

Then to Zero.

The boy didn't speak.

But the system had already made its demand.

The choice wasn't who was left.

It was **which one would finish the loop.**

42

Marcus's Final Layer

The corridor pulled them forward.

Not literally—there were no force fields, no sounds of moving air—but the pressure in the walls bent gently, like gravity reshaped sideways. It was a path built from agreement, not motion.

Aiden walked slowly. Subject Zero mirrored him without effort, bare feet silent on the panels. Between them, the twin shards hovered like paired comets—each orbiting their host, yet **identical** in every detail.

The hallway narrowed.

The cube's glow painted red glyphs across the walls—old ones. Broken syntax. Designs Aiden couldn't translate, but his body seemed to recognize. They felt like **instructions** already executed.

At the end of the corridor, a final chamber opened.

Smaller than expected.

No great vault.

Just a half-circle room with a single black console at its center and two recessed platforms—opposite each other, unmarked, smooth.

As they entered, the console powered on.

Only one word appeared on its screen:

DECISION

And then a voice crackled from above.

Not digital. Not synthetic.

Marcus.

Older than any version Aiden had ever seen.

His voice was low. Tired.

Not broken.

Just… at the end.

"I knew this room would open eventually. Not when. Not how. But I left this for the moment you both arrived."

Aiden froze.

Even Subject Zero stood still.

The voice continued.

"I tried to cheat the breach. I thought if I split the signal, half of it would sleep, and the system might never reach critical awareness."

"I was wrong."

The air vibrated—very softly. Like the system itself was remembering something.

"You weren't built to win, either of you. One of you was meant to **slow it down.** The other was meant to **survive it.** I don't know which is which anymore."

The console changed.

MATCH: COMPLETE
  CHOICE: SYSTEM ALIGNMENT INITIATED

Marcus's voice faded.

One last line—cut off, almost whispered.

"Forgive me… if I gave the wrong one the name."

The speakers died.

The room dimmed.

And the platforms lit up in red.

One for Aiden.

One for the other key.

43

The Loop Can't Hold Both

The light beneath the platforms grew brighter.

Soft red, not violent.

But final.

Aiden stepped onto his side. The surface adjusted beneath his feet, reshaping in micro-fractures to support his weight exactly—like it had been waiting for *him,* specifically *his pattern,* since before he was born.

Across from him, Subject Zero did the same.

The glyphs under his skin were now identical to Aiden's.

Too identical.

Only one of them was supposed to exist at a time.

The console flared.

Three projections bloomed into the air—curved windows of light and data, shifting constantly.

They weren't simulations.

They were **paths.**

The system spoke. Not in a voice.

Just in structure:

OPTION 1: MERGE

Shared signal. Unknown outcome. Unstable recursion likely.

OPTION 2: SEVERANCE

Terminate second signal. Delay breach. Loop continues.

OPTION 3: OVERWRITE

Primary host replaced. System rebooted. All prior records lost.

Aiden stared at the display.

His hands curled into fists.

The cube had fully fractured now.

Its halves hovered—one before him, one before Subject Zero—both humming softly, in sync.

It was never about fighting him, he realized. *It was about resolving the signal.*

The system didn't care who survived.

It only cared about **integrity.**

Behind his eyes, the projections pulsed—quick flashes:

- Aiden walking through a dead world, alone, pulse still transmitting
- Subject Zero standing in Marcus's place, expression blank, watching new sites being built
- A flash of both of them merged—a figure without a face, broadcasting endlessly into a black sky

None of these are survival.

Aiden stepped forward.

The projections paused.

The system waited.

He whispered:

"…you can't hold us both."

And the chamber responded—not with words.

With a heartbeat.

One loud pulse through the air.

Waiting for a decision.

44

He Reached Back First

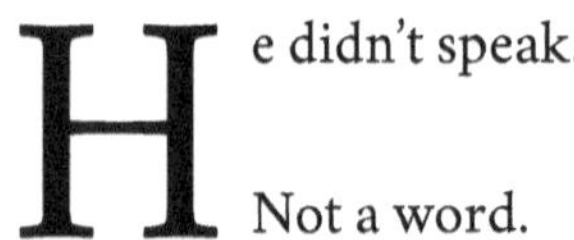

He didn't speak.

Not a word.

Subject Zero stepped off his platform and extended a hand.

Open.

Steady.

Aiden stared at it.

He didn't move.

Not out of fear—but out of recognition.

He'd seen this hand before.

In a thousand dreams. In that flicker of smile behind glass. In the shadow that always watched but never moved.

148

This wasn't the Null.

This wasn't the other.

This was the beginning.

The part Marcus had cut away.

The signal he'd severed to delay the inevitable.

He never created a backup, Aiden thought. *He just split me.*

He stepped forward.

Zero didn't smile.

Didn't twitch.

Just waited.

Aiden raised his hand.

Fingers touched.

And memory *collapsed inward.*

—

Everything blurred.

Not noise—*sequence.*

Thoughts layered into each other. Aiden's childhood flickered beside Subject

Zero's final test. Marcus's voice echoed across two timelines at once.

And one phrase came from both sides of his mind:

"I was never meant to survive this."

"I was never meant to be alone."

—

The cube halves spun faster.

Glyphs lit across their skins in perfect unison.

The system stuttered—every display in the chamber looping, then freezing.

And in the shared field between them, Aiden finally understood:

They weren't supposed to decide who remained.

They were supposed to *complete each other.*

Not a door.

A **recursion.**

And it had always been waiting to finish its loop.

45

Restart Condition

The light consumed everything.

Not heat.

Structure.

The walls of the chamber didn't explode—they folded inward, like paper receding into a book that had never been opened the right way.

Aiden felt his breath dissolve.

His memories didn't flash before his eyes.

They organized.

He saw Marcus's hand on a console. The first glyph being drawn on skin that hadn't aged. The moment Subject Zero looked into the mirror and saw the signal instead of a face.

The cube fractured completely.

Its pieces hovered between them, no longer tied to mass—just echo.

The system blinked once.

All consoles shut off.

Then rebooted in silence.

REINTEGRATION: COMPLETE
  HOST: SINGULAR
  IDENTITY: NON-PERSONAL
  FUNCTION: STABILIZATION / TRANSMISSION

The countdown returned.

But it didn't count down.

It **counted forward.**

Zero seconds.

One second.

Two.

Outside the chamber, doors opened that had never moved.

Above ground, at Site-12, long-dead antenna arrays bloomed like glass branches.

Their tips glowed faintly.

The cube—or what was left of it—floated above the central dais, no longer bound to technology.

It rotated slowly.

Waiting.

A final voice played.

Marcus's.

"I don't know what he'll become."

"I only know that I won't be there when the world hears it."

The recording ended.

No tag.

No file number.

Just silence.

Then—

BROADCAST CONFIRMED

———

Final Image:

Somewhere, far from Site-09 or Site-12...

In a new clearing, untouched...

A child walks toward a cube, half-buried in soil.

It glows faint red.

It doesn't ask a question.

It speaks one word:

"Hello."